PARENTS AND CAREGIVERS,

Stone Arch Readers are designed to provide enjoyable reading experiences, as well as opportunities to develop vocabulary, literacy skills, and comprehension. Here are a few ways to support your beginning reader:

- Talk with your child about the ideas addressed in the story.

- Discuss each illustration, mentioning the characters, where they are, and what they are doing.

- Read with expression, pointing to each word. You may want to read the whole story through and then revisit parts of the story to ensure that the meanings of words or phrases are understood.

- Talk about why the character did what he or she did and what your child would do in that situation.

- Help your child connect with characters and events in the story.

Remember, reading with your child should be fun, not forced. Each moment spent reading with your child is a priceless investment in his or her literacy life.

GAIL SAUNDERS-SMITH, PH.D.

STONE ARCH READERS

are published by Stone Arch Books
151 Good Counsel Drive, P.O. Box 669
Mankato, Minnesota 56002
www.stonearchbooks.com

Copyright © 2010 by Stone Arch Books

Library of Congress
Cataloging-in-Publication Data
Meister, Cari.
 Moopy, the underground monster /
by Cari Meister; illustrated by Dennis Messner.
  p. cm. – (Stone arch readers)
 ISBN 978-1-4342-1630-4 (library binding)
 ISBN 978-1-4342-1745-5 (paperback)
 [1. Hospitality–Fiction. 2. Monsters–Fiction.]
I. Messner, Dennis, ill. II. Title.
 PZ7.M515916Moo 2010
 [E]–dc22   2009000889

Summary: Moopy, who likes being alone, gets a visitor.

Creative Director: Heather Kindseth
Designer: Bob Lentz

Reading Consultants:
Gail Saunders-Smith, Ph.D.
Melinda Melton Crow, M.Ed.
Laurie K. Holland, Media Specialist

MOOPY
THE UNDERGROUND
MONSTER

BY CARI MEISTER

ILLUSTRATED BY
DENNIS MESSNER

STONE ARCH BOOKS
MINNEAPOLIS   SAN DIEGO

This is Moopy. She does not have eyes. She does not need them. She lives underground in the dark.

She has sharp claws. They are good for digging.

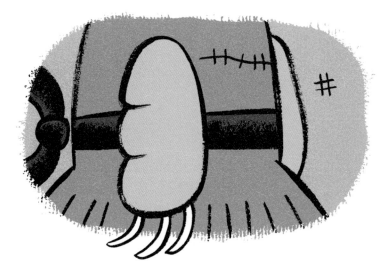

She has a big nose. It is good for smelling.

Moopy lives alone. She likes it that way. No one tells her what to do.

She eats what she wants.
She stays up late. She dances
to loud music.

Tonight, Moopy is making dinner. There is a knock at the door.

"Please let me in," says
a voice.

Moopy never lets anyone in.
She sticks her nose out the hole.
She sniffs. It is another monster.

"Go away," Moopy says.

"I have walked a long way," says the monster. "I am hungry and tired."

Moopy is not mean, but she likes to be alone.

"You cannot come in, but you can have this," says Moopy.

"Thank you," says the
monster.

In the morning, Moopy finds the empty plate. She also finds a ring.

"How nice," she says.

That night, Moopy dances to
loud music. There is a knock at
the door.

Moopy sticks her nose out the
hole. She sniffs.

It is the same monster.

"There is no room," says Moopy.
"Go away."

"I am hungry and tired," says
the monster.

"You can have these blankets," she says.

"Thank you," says the monster.

The next morning, Moopy
finds the blankets. She finds
some flowers, too.

Then Moopy goes digging for food.

Moopy digs all day, but she does not find any food. Then she hears a loud noise.

Dirt and rocks fall on Moopy.
All of her digging made too
many holes.

Her bed is broken. Her home
is gone.

Moopy is hungry. She is tired.
She has no place to go.

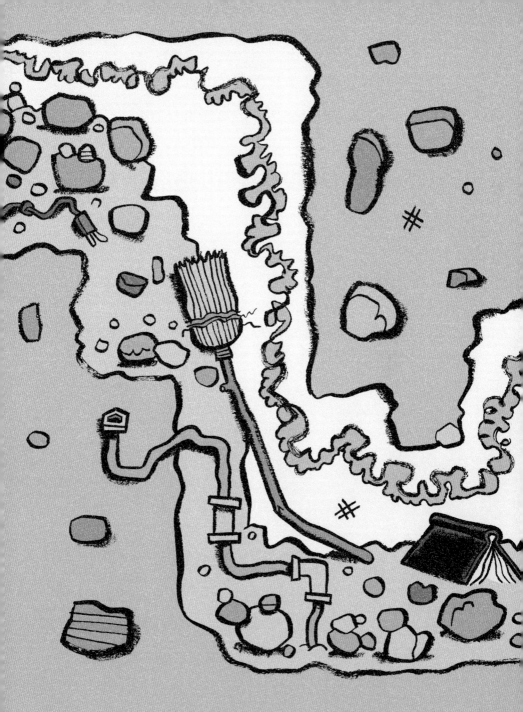

Then Moopy smells something
good. She follows the smell.

"Welcome to my new home," says the monster. "Thanks for being so nice to me before. Would you like some dinner?"

THE END

STORY WORDS

underground   hungry

smelling   tired

knock   blankets

sniffs   Total Word Count: 320

MEET ALL FOUR OF OUR MONSTERS!